THESE AREN'T ORDINA...

MONSTER HEROES

by
Blake Hoena

illustrated by
Dave Bardin

Capstone Young Readers
a capstone imprint

Monster Heroes is published by
Capstone Young Readers, a Capstone Imprint
1710 Roe Crest Drive
North Mankato, Minnesota 56003
www.mycapstone.com

Library of Congress Cataloging-in-Publication data
is available on the Library of Congress website.

ISBN: 978-1-62370-783-5 (paperback)

Summary: Linda (the witch), Brian (the zombie), Will (the ghost), and
Mina (the vampire) are monsters who fight for good. While other monsters
try to hurt people, these four Monster Heroes help people. From switching
potions to feeding zombies, these monsters will do whatever it takes
to stop the monster madness caused by other creatures.

Book design by Ted Williams

Photo credits: Shutterstock: kasha_malasha,
design element, popular business, design element

Printed and bound in China.
010104S17

TABLE OF
CONTENTS

MINA *(the Vampire)*

Mina thinks people taste like dirty socks, so beet juice is her snack of choice. Its red color has fooled her parents into thinking that she's a traditional blood-sucking vampire instead of a superhero hopeful. She has the ability to change into a bat or a mouse at will.

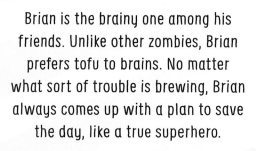

Brian is the brainy one among his friends. Unlike other zombies, Brian prefers tofu to brains. No matter what sort of trouble is brewing, Brian always comes up with a plan to save the day, like a true superhero.

BRIAN *(the Zombie)*

WILL *(the Ghost)*

Will is quite shy. Luckily he can turn invisible any time he wants because he is a ghost. When Will is doing good deeds, he likes to remain unseen. His invisibility helps him act brave like a real superhero.

With a wave of her wand and a poetic chant, Linda can reverse any magical curse. She hopes to use her magic to help people, just like a superhero would.

LINDA *(the Witch)*

STORY 1:

THE GHOST TRAP

BULLY GHOSTS

Will hurried through the crowded halls of Frankenstein Elementary. He was on his way to his computer class. As always, he was running late.

He zipped around a werewolf. He zoomed through an ogre. Then he floated over a mummy.

In the classroom, Will saw Jim, Scott, and Kip. They were scary ghosts. Even though Will was a ghost, he didn't like to scare people.

Will and his friends weren't like other monsters. They didn't scare people or haunt houses. His friends wanted to be superheroes and save the day.

Will sat down in front of the other ghosts. As he waited for his computer to turn on, he listened to them.

"A new family moved into the old Hill House," Jim said.

"That's the place by the cemetery, right?" Scott asked.

"Yeah, across from Shirley Jackson's tomb," Kip added.

Just then, Will's computer beeped. The other ghosts stopped talking. Will looked back. They were staring at him.

"Should we ask Will to join us?" Jim asked.

Scott shook his head no. "He's a scaredy-cat."

"Yeah! He couldn't even scare a cat, either," Kip added.

The three ghosts moaned loudly. That's what ghosts did when they thought something was funny.

"Wh-wh-where are you going?" Will asked.

"To the Hill House," Scott said.

"Yeah, to haunt some people," Jim added.

"Want to come?" Kip asked.

"N-n-no," Will whispered. He turned back to his computer.

"That's what I thought," Scott said.

Will couldn't let the mean ghosts haunt people. He rushed to meet his friends at lunch. He knew they could help him.

SUPER MONSTER FRIENDS

At lunch, Will sat with his friends. Brian munched on a tofu brainwich. Mina slurped some beet juice. And Linda ate something too disgusting and smelly to describe.

Will told them about Jim, Scott, and Kip.

"They want to scare the people who moved into the old Hill House," Will said. "And they are going to do it soon."

"We can't let them do that," Linda said.

"We need a plan," Brian said.

The friends thought and ate.

Then they ate some more and

thought some more.

"What are ghosts afraid of?"

Brian asked.

"People laughter," Will said.

"What?" Linda said in surprise.

"No way!" Mina shouted.

"Like chuckles and giggles?" Brian asked.

Will nodded. He said, "Ghosts like to scare people to hear them shout and scream. But when people laugh, they sound creepy. Ghosts think that's scary."

"That's so weird! But it does give me an idea," Brian said.

The friends leaned in as Brian told them his plan. As always, Brian came up with the perfect idea.

That afternoon, the friends met at their secret hideout. It was a tree house high up in the branches of a big old oak tree. The tree grew in the middle of the cemetery.

"Are you sure the plan will work?" Will asked.

He was nervous. He didn't want to make the mean ghosts mad.

Brian lumbered over to Will. He put an arm around the ghost.

"Don't worry," Brian said. "It will definitely make people laugh."

CHAPTER 3

SOCKS AND UNDERPANTS

The friends headed over to the old Hill House and hid. A few minutes later, they saw Jim, Scott, and Kip.

"Are you ready, Will?" Brian whispered.

Will nodded and then floated over to the mean ghosts.

"Can I join you?" Will asked.

"The more the scarier," Scott moaned.

The ghosts floated through one of the walls in the house. Once they were out of sight, Will's friends went into action.

Poof! Mina changed into a bat. She flew through a window into the laundry room. Brian lumbered over to the door. He got ready to push the doorbell.

Linda waved her wand. She chanted, "Creakity creak, stay sound asleep until you hear the ding-a-ling of the doorbell ring!" Then she cast her spell. *Bam*!

Inside the house, the people fell asleep and snored loudly.

"*Ahhhoooooo*," Jim groaned.

"*Booga-booga-booga!*" Scott shouted.

"*Eeeeeeeeeee,*" Kip screeched.

No one in the house stirred. All the ghosts could hear were people snoring in the rooms above.

Will floated over to where Mina was hiding in the laundry room. He grabbed a basket of dirty socks and underpants that Mina had found.

"Try putting these on," Will said to the mean ghosts. "It will be really scary."

Just then, the doorbell rang, and the people woke up. At the top of the stairs stood a boy and a girl. Jim, Scott, and Kip turned to scare the kids.

But ghosts are invisible. All the kids saw were socks and underpants floating in the air.

The kids giggled and chuckled and snorted with laughter.

"Oh, no!" Jim shouted. "Not laughing!"

"Ahhhh!" Scott screamed. "People laughter is so scary!"

"Let's get out of here!" Kip yelled.

The ghosts dashed through a wall and disappeared into the night. Will joined his friends at the front door.

"Just like superheroes, we saved the day!" Linda said.

"We sure did! Now let's get out of here," Brian said. "This place is seriously creepy!"

STORY 2:

VAMPIRES AND VEGGIES

BEET JUICE

Slurp! Mina took a big sip from a glass filled with red liquid.

"Is that blood?" Linda gasped.

"Of course not! It's just beet juice," Mina said.

"Ew, that's worse," Linda said. She scrunched up her nose in disgust. "Why do you drink *that*?"

"I drink beet juice so my parents think I drink blood," Mina said. "You know, like a normal vampire."

"Well, it fooled me," Linda said.

"At least it doesn't taste as bad as people do," Mina said.

"Really?" Linda asked. "What do people taste like?"

"Like dirty socks soaked in pickle juice," Mina said.

"Double ew!" Linda said.

Just then, the doorbell rang. Mina and Linda ran to the top of the staircase to see who was at the front door.

It was the new neighbors. Mina's parents greeted two adults.

A boy stood in front of the adults. He was about Mina's age. The boy looked up and waved to the girls.

"We're so glad you could make it," Mina's dad said with an evil grin.

"Yes, we love having people for dinner," Mina's mom said with a matching evil grin.

The girls ran back to Mina's room.

"No, no, no!" Mina said. "This is bad. Really, *really* bad."

"Why? Don't you like having dinner guests?" Linda asked.

"You don't understand," Mina said. "They are not dinner guests. They *are* dinner!"

"Oh!" Linda gulped.

"We better call Will and Brian," Mina said.

DINNER GUESTS

"Mina!" Mina's mom called. "We need you to come down."

The girls looked at each other, worried. Their friends hadn't arrived yet.

"What should I do?" Mina asked.

Linda shrugged. "I don't know."

"Mina," Mina's dad called. "Come meet Mr. and Mrs. Plasma and their son, Greg."

"I have to go," Mina said.

"When Brian and Will get here," Linda whispered, "we'll think of a plan to save your neighbors. Try to stall."

Mina slowly walked down the stairs. Her parents waited at the bottom. They looked extra excited.

"Hi," the boy said. He seemed very friendly.

"Hey," Mina replied, trying to act normal.

"Mina, please show Greg around," Mina's dad said.

"You should go get a bite to eat in the kitchen," Mina's mom said with a wink.

Mina grabbed Greg's hand. She pulled him into the kitchen.

"Your parents are kind of strange," Greg said. "They keep asking about my blood type and if I take garlic supplements."

Mina sat Greg down at a table. She took a deep breath. She was afraid Greg would think she was a blood-sucking monster too. But she had to warn him about her family.

"We're vampires," Mina whispered.
Then she grinned, to show him
her pointy fangs.

"That's cool!" Greg said.

"You're not afraid?" Mina asked.

"No, not all monsters are scary," Greg said. "My best friend at my old school is a werewolf."

"Yeah, some of us are different," Mina said with a smile.

There was a tap on the kitchen window. It was Will. Mina opened the window to let him in.

"This is my friend Will," Mina said to Greg.

In one hand, Will carried Mina's glass of beet juice.

"Is that blood?" Greg asked.

"No, silly. It's beet juice," Mina said. "I don't drink blood. I'm a vegetarian."

"She drinks beet juice so her parents won't know her secret," Will said.

"Why can't your parents know you don't drink blood?" Greg asked, confused.

"My parents would never understand. They are traditional vampires," Mina said.

"We aren't like other monsters," Will said. "We like to help people."

"Like superheroes?" Greg asked.

"Exactly. We need everyone to think we are scary monsters," Mina said. "Then we can secretly help people."

"Enough talking," Will said. He held up a red marker.

"What's that for?" Greg asked.

"It's part of our plan to save you and your parents," Will said. "And to keep Mina's secret a secret."

Will floated over to Greg. With the marker, he drew two red dots on Greg's neck.

"Perfect!" Will said. "Now I'd better go before Mina's parents see me."

"Thanks, Will!" Mina said.

"Happy to help," Will said as he floated out the window and disappeared.

PIZZA PLEASE

Just then, Mina's parents entered the kitchen. They looked at the red marks on Greg's neck. They saw Mina sipping her beet juice and smiled.

"I hope you are enjoying your snack," Mina's mom said.

"Now it's time for our dinner," Mina's dad said.

Before they could start dinner, the doorbell rang. Mina and Greg poked their heads out of the kitchen to watch.

Will and Linda watched from the top of the stairs, hoping their plan would work.

When the door opened, their friend Brian stepped inside.

"Pizza delivery!" he shouted.

Mina's parents looked confused.

"I guess we're having pizza for dinner," Mina's dad said.

"Your plan worked!" Mina said.

"Of course it did," Brian said.

"And we made a new friend," Linda said.

Will and Greg could only nod
and mumble. They were too busy
stuffing their faces with pizza.

STORY 3:

WITCH'S BREW

CHAPTER 1

A FAMILIAR PROBLEM

"*Peep*! *Peep*!"

"What is it, Petey?" Linda asked her pet caterpillar.

All witches had a familiar. This special pet helped them do witchy stuff. Witches understood their familiars even though they didn't talk.

Petey peeped again.

"Oh, no!" Linda gasped. "Griselda and Agnes are using Mom's cauldron!"

"*Squeak*!" Petey squealed. That meant yes.

Linda ran to the kitchen and peeked in. Her sisters and their familiars circled a large, black cauldron. Griselda had a black cat named Scratch. Agnes had a snake named Slither.

"They must be brewing a potion," Linda whispered to Petey.

"Eye of newt and toe of frog," Griselda cackled.

"Wing of bat and tongue of dog," Agnes screeched.

"Double, double toil and trouble," Griselda chanted.

"Fire burn and caldron bubble," Agnes sang.

Agnes threw something into the pot. *Bam*!

"*Eek*!" Linda squealed in fear.

Her sisters turned to Linda.

"What are *you* doing here?" Griselda asked.

"Go away! You'll ruin our potion — again," Agnes said.

Griselda stepped in front of the pot as Agnes pushed Linda out of the room.

"But I —" Linda tried to say.

Bang! The kitchen door slammed shut.

Linda ran back to her room. She knew her sisters were up to no good. She needed help!

Linda called her friends. They were always up for a new adventure. "Meet me at our secret hideout," she told her friends.

SUPER FRIENDS

Linda and Petey rushed to the cemetery. They found the tall oak tree and quickly climbed up. Then they crawled through a trap door leading into their hideout.

Inside, Mina and Will were waiting. Linda did not see Brian. Zombies were always late.

As they waited for Brian, Linda
told her friends about her sisters'
new potion.

"What does it do?" Mina asked.

Linda shrugged. "I don't know."

"I bet it's something horrible," Will said.

"I *know* it's something horrible," Linda said.

"That's why we can't let them use their potion," Brian said as he climbed up the ladder into the hideout.

Everyone agreed.

"We need to know their plan," Brian said.

"But they won't let me near the potion," Linda said.

"I can spy on them," Mina said. *Poof!* Mina turned into a bat.

"Awesome," Brian said.

"I'll be right back," Mina the bat squeaked. She fluttered out the window and flew away.

The others waited and waited and waited. When Mina the bat returned, she changed back into her vampire form. *Poof!*

"Awesome," Brian said again.

"What are they doing?" Linda asked.

"They are setting up a lemonade stand," Mina explained.

"*Peep! Peep!*" Petey squeaked.

"I know, Petey," Linda said. "They didn't use any lemons in their potion. Not one."

"Then why would your sisters set up a lemonade stand?" Mina asked.

"To trick people into drinking their potion," Linda said. "The potion must do something bad to them."

"That's horrible," Will said with a shudder.

"We need to stop them," Brian said.

"Then let's go!" Linda said.

The friends climbed down from the hideout and ran to Linda's house.

THAT'S NOT LEMONADE

Griselda and Agnes were in the front yard. They sat at a table with the bubbling cauldron. Linda and her friends hid behind a bush.

"Listen up! I have a plan," Linda said. "But first, I need a real lemon."

"Where are we going to find one of those?" Brian asked.

Mina dug into her pocket. She
pulled out a bright yellow lemon.

"Why did you have a lemon in
your pocket?" Brian asked.

"I like sucking on them," Mina
said with a smile.

Following Linda's plan, Brian walked over to the lemonade stand.

"Hmmm," he said. "I don't know what to order."

"All we have is lemonade," Agnes said.

"Yeah, just lemonade," Griselda said.

Mina changed into a mouse. She ran across the sidewalk to keep people away.

Will had taken off his sheet. He was now invisible. He carried the lemon to the cauldron and dropped it into the pot.

Linda quietly chanted, "Lemon!
Lemon! Yellow and bright. Give
my sisters a nasty fright."

Bam!

"What happened?" Agnes
coughed.

"I don't know," Griselda said.

"Um, I don't think I'm thirsty anymore," Brian said as he quickly ran off.

Mina turned back into a vampire. All of the friends hid behind the bush again. They watched as smoke spread out from the witch's brew.

"I think something's wrong," Griselda said to Agnes.

"You think?" Agnes said, annoyed.

Critters were gathering all around the sisters. Mice scurried along the ground. Squirrels scampered through the trees.

"Those critters look really hungry," Agnes said.

"The potion was supposed to turn people into animals so we could roast them for supper," Griselda shrieked.

"Not make animals want to turn *us* into dinner," Agnes cried.

The sisters screamed and ran away. The animals chased after them at full speed.

Linda and her friends laughed.

"We saved the day," Will said.

"We make a great team," Linda said.

Everyone agreed.

STORY 4:

ZOMBIES AND MEATBALLS

BRAINS OR BRIAN?

Brian was at his desk working when he heard a strange noise.

"*Braaaiiins!*" came a loud moan.

Brian glanced around his room.

"Did someone just say my name?" Brian whispered.

"*Braaaiiins!*" came the moan again. Only this time, it was louder.

Brian looked up from his homework. He was getting annoyed. He was also getting a little scared.

"Who keeps calling my name?" he asked out loud.

His friends were always saying he studied too much. Maybe they were outside trying to scare him.

"Knock it off you guys," Brian said. "I'm trying to study."

When the moaning continued, Brian realized it wasn't his friends. He went over to his window and looked outside. What he saw scared him more than the moaning.

"Oh, no!" he gasped.

Zombies were everywhere! Hundreds of them lumbered and stumbled about. They destroyed everything in their path, including plants, trees, and mailboxes.

"*Braaaiiins!*" they moaned.

Brian knew that a horde of hungry zombies could be a danger to anyone with a brain.

"*Braaaiiins!*" they moaned louder.

"They are saying *Braaaiiins* not *Briiiaaan,*" Brian said. "It's true what people say about zombies — they really are hard to understand!"

Brian needed to take action, and he had to do it fast.

He made his way downstairs and peeked outside. More and more zombies filled the streets.

"What is going on?" Brian asked quietly. "The other zombies are usually so well behaved."

"*Braaaiiins!*" they moaned.

Then Brian saw the problem.

Down the block was Tofu Brains Deli & Coffee Shop. A CLOSED sign hung outside.

"That's it! They are all hungry!" Brian said.

"*Braaaiiins!*" the zombies moaned.

"I need to call my friends," Brian said. "We need to meet at our hideout right away!"

CHAPTER

2

WHERE ARE THE BRAINS?

Brian's friends were smart, funny, and kind. He knew they would help him.

Brian lumbered to the cemetery and climbed up to the hideout. His friends were already there.

Mina hung upside down in one corner. Will floated in another corner. Linda sat in a chair with her pet caterpillar sitting on her shoulder.

"What's wrong?" Linda asked Brian.

"The Tofu Brains Deli & Coffee Shop closed," Brian said.

"No way!" Mina shouted. "I loved that place."

"So did I, but why is that such a big problem?" Will asked. "There are other places to eat."

"But that's where all the zombies eat. Now they are hungry," Brian said. "They are forming a horde."

His friend's eyes went wide with fear. Sure, zombies were slow and clumsy. But a horde of them was unstoppable. They would eat and destroy everything in their path.

"They will look for anyone or anything with a brain," Brian said. "And then . . ."

"This *is* a big problem!" Will said.

"It sure is!" Brian said.

Mina held up a map of the city.

"Where do you think they will go?" she asked.

"That's easy," Brian said. "Frankenstein Elementary School has the most brains in town."

Brian looked at the map. He put a finger on Zombie Town. Then he traced the streets leading to the elementary school.

"This is the path they will follow," Brian said.

"How do we stop the horde from getting there?" Will asked.

Brian studied the map. There were stores and restaurants along the way to the school.

"That's it!" Brian said.

"What's it?" Linda asked.

"A trip to the meatball shop, that's what!" Brian said.

"Getting a bite to eat?" Mina said. "That's your brilliant plan?"

"Just trust me," Brian said.

MEATBALL BRAINS

The friends stood outside Randy's Meatball Sandwich Shop.

"The meatballs here are really good," Will said.

"And they kind of look like little brains," Brian said, holding one up. "Now, huddle up, team!"

Brian whispered his plan. They all agreed and got into position.

Linda waved her wand at the restaurant's sign.

"Your name must change," she chanted.

Poof! The sign now read Igor's Meatball Brainwich Shop. Linda's job was done.

Now it was Brian's turn. He joined the zombie horde.

"*Braaaiiins!*" the zombies moaned as they lumbered down the street.

"*Meeeatbaaalls!*" Brian groaned.

"*Braaaiiins!*" the zombies moaned again.

"*Meeeatbaaalls!*" Brian groaned louder.

The zombies kept moaning. Brian kept groaning louder. Soon, the zombies' moans changed to groans. Brian's job was done.

"*Meeeatbaaalls!*" the zombies groaned.

Will tied a string to a meatball. Then he took off his sheet. Now he was invisible.

Will used the meatball on a string to lead the zombies to the sandwich shop. Will pulled the meatball away as soon as the zombies reached for it.

"*Meeeatbaaalls!*" the zombies groaned.

Brian groaned along with them. "*Meeeatbaaalls!*"

Brian and the zombies followed Will right to the restaurant. Will's job was done. Now it was Mina's turn to take over.

Mina quickly made stacks and stacks of meatball sandwiches. Then she changed into a bat. She fluttered about the restaurant.

The horde of zombies entered the shop and attacked the piles of meatball sandwiches.

"*Meeeatbaaalls!*" the zombies groaned.

The friends regrouped outside the sub shop. They watched as zombies ate every last sandwich in sight.

"We stopped them!" Linda said.

"The Monster Heroes saved the day again," Mina said.

"That's because we make a great team," Brian said.

"We sure do," Will mumbled between bites. "What? Nobody else is hungry?"

DAVE BARDIN

Dave Bardin studied illustration at Cal State Fullerton while working as an art teacher. As an artist, Dave has worked on many different projects for television, books, comics, and animation. In his spare time Dave enjoys watching documentaries, listening to podcasts, traveling, and spending time with friends and family. He works out of Los Angeles, California.

BLAKE HOENA

Blake A. Hoena grew up in central Wisconsin, where he wrote stories about robots conquering the moon and trolls lumbering around the woods behind his parents' house. He now lives in Minnesota and continues to write about fun things like space aliens and superheroes. Blake has written more than fifty chapter books and graphic novels for children.